Interesting Elephants

Written by
Laura Appleton-Smith and Susan Blackaby

Laura Appleton-Smith was born and raised in Vermont and holds a degree in English from Middlebury College. Laura is a primary school teacher who has combined her talents in creative writing and her experience in early childhood education to create *Books to Remember*. Laura lives in New Hampshire with her husband, Terry.

Susan Blackaby has worked in educational publishing for over 30 years. In addition to her writing curriculum, she is the author of *Rembrandt's Hat* (Houghton Mifflin, 2002); *Cleopatra: Egypt's Last and Greatest Queen* (Sterling, 2009); *Nest, Nook, and Cranny* (Charlesbridge, 2010), winner of the 2011 Lion and the Unicorn Award for Excellence in North American Poetry; and *Brownie Groundhog and the February Fox* (Sterling, 2011). She lives in Portland, Oregon.

A Book to Remember™
Published by Flyleaf Publishing

For orders or information, contact us at **(800) 449-7006**.
Please visit our website at **www.flyleafpublishing.com**

First Edition 10/12
Library of Congress Control Number: 2012939857
ISBN-13: 978-1-60541-145-3
Printed and bound in the USA at Worzalla Publishing, Stevens Point, WI. 10/12

For my wonderful mother, Carol.

LAS

To the Red-Tailed Readers.

SB

1 bushel x 23 = 23 bushels

What animal can munch 23 bushels of grasses and trees...

1 gallon x 50 = 50 gallons

and drink up to 50 gallons of water each day?

If you said an African elephant, you are correct!
This is an African elephant.

Trunk

Ear

Tusk

Legs

4

The Biggest Land Mammal

African elephants are the biggest
land mammals on the planet.

African elephants can be up to 11 feet tall!

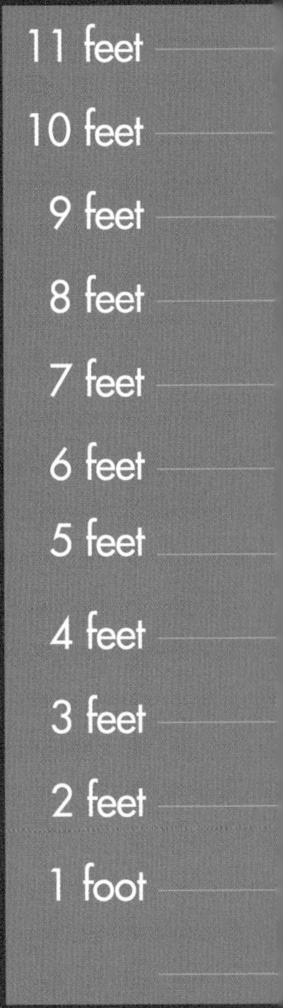

11 feet

10 feet

9 feet

8 feet

7 feet

6 feet

5 feet

4 feet

3 feet

2 feet

1 foot

This elephant
is 11 feet tall.

This man is
6 feet tall.

6

African Elephant Habitat

The habitat of the African elephant is
the tropical jungles and grasslands of Africa.

Africa

■ African Elephant Habitat

Equator

N
nw · ne
W   E
sw · se
S

Elephants travel within their habitat.

When the West African summer gets arid,
or when it is hot and there is little water,
elephants must travel to a river that has water
for them to drink.

Elephant Herds

A herd is a big pack of animals that feed and travel with each other.

Elephants travel in herds. There can be up to a hundred elephants in a single herd.

An Elephant's Trunk

Elephants have long trunks that are strong and skilled. An elephant can use its trunk to stretch up and grab a tree branch or to pick up the littlest strand of grass.

Sunscreen?

An elephant's trunk can suck up water, too.

On hot days, an elephant can swish water over its body.

Then the elephant adds dust to its wet skin.

The mud from the mix of water and dust

acts like sunscreen!

Elephant Talk

Elephants can also use their trunks to trumpet, or "talk," to each other. This trumpeting is like elephant yelling.

An elephant can "talk" in a soft, deep rumble. This rumbling is like elephant whisper-talking.

Interesting Elephants

African elephants are fantastic tree-munching, water-swishing, trunk-stretching, trumpet-talking, whisper-rumbling animals.

Aren't elephants interesting?

Tree Munching

Water Swishing

Trunk Stretching

Trumpet Talking

Whisper Rumbling

Glossary

bushel
A way to measure some dry foods like corn, wheat, and apples.
A bushel is the same amount as 8 gallons.

gallon
A way to measure liquids like milk and water.
A gallon is the same amount as 4 quarts.

mammal
A warm-blooded animal with a backbone that has hair or fur on its skin.
Mammal mothers produce milk to feed their babies.

tropical
Having to do with the tropics, or places near the equator,
where the climate is hot and wet.

jungle

A wild tropical forest filled with many trees and plants.

grassland

A large area of land covered mostly with grasses.

habitat

The natural home environment, or place, where a plant or animal lives.

Prerequisite Skills

Single consonants and short vowels
Final double consonants **ff**, **gg**, **ll**, **nn**, **ss**, **tt**, **zz**
Consonant /k/ **ck**
Consonant digraphs /ng/ **ng**, /th/ **th**, /hw/ **wh**
Schwa /ə/ **a, e, i, o, u**
Long /ē/ **ee, y**
r-Controlled /ûr/ **er**
Variant vowel /aw/ **al, all**
Consonant /l/ **le**
/d/ or /t/ **–ed**

Prerequisite Skills are foundational phonics skills that have been previously introduced.

Target Letter-Sound Correspondence is the letter-sound correspondence introduced in the story.

High-Frequency Puzzle Words are high-frequency irregular words.

Story Puzzle Words are irregular words that are not high frequency.

Decodable Words are words that can be decoded solely on the basis of the letter-sound correspondences or phonetic elements that have been introduced.

Target Letter-Sound Correspondence	
Digraph /th/ sound spelled **th**	
that	this
the	with
them	within
then	

Target Letter-Sound Correspondence	
Digraph /ng/ sound spelled **ng, n**	
drink	swishing
interesting	talking
jungles	trumpeting
long	trunk
rumbling	trunks
single	yelling
strong	

Target Letter-Sound Correspondence	
Digraph /ch/ sound spelled **ch, tch**	
branch	stretch
munch	stretching
munching	

Target Letter-Sound Correspondence	
Digraph /f/ sound spelled **ph**	
elephant	elephants
elephant's	

Target Letter-Sound Correspondence	
Digraph /sh/ sound spelled **sh**	
swish	swishing

Target Letter-Sound Correspondence	
Digraph /hw/ sound spelled **wh**	
when	whisper

Story Puzzle Words

aren't   bushels
bushel

High-Frequency Puzzle Words

also	or
are	other
be	over
day	said
days	their
each	there
for	to
from	too
have	use
like	what
of	you

Decodable Words

1	correct	if	rumble
6	deep	in	skilled
11	dust	is	skin
23	fantastic	it	soft
50	feed	its	strand
a	feet	land	suck
acts	gallon	little	summer
adds	gallons	littlest	sunscreen
Africa	gets	mammal	talk
African	grab	mammals	tall
an	grass	man	travel
and	grasses	mix	tree
animal	grasslands	mud	trees
animals	habitat	must	tropical
arid	has	on	trumpet
big	herd	pack	up
biggest	herds	pick	water
body	hot	planet	west
can	hundred	river	wet

24